E HIN   3/99
Hindley, Judy.
    The best thing about a
puppy   10 99

DATE DUE

MAR 2 0 '99	OC 08 01		
AP 17 '99	DE 21 01		
AP 30 '99	JY 1 0 '02		
MAY 1 7 '99	AG -1 '02		
MY 27 '99	OC 16 '02		
JE -9 '99	MR 10 03		
JE 19 '99	MAR 2 0 2003		
JY 13 '99	OCT 2 2003		
AUG 1 0 '00	NO 19 03		
MY -7 '01	MAR 1 8 2004		
JY 26 '01	APR 1 6 2004		
	DEC 1 2004		
AG 15 01			

With thanks to Kate Weller! **J. H.**

For Rosina **P. C.**

Text copyright © 1998 by Judy Hindley
Illustrations copyright © 1998 by Patricia Casey

First U.S. edition 1998

Library of Congress Cataloging-in-Publication Data

Hindley, Judy.
The best thing about a puppy / Judy Hindley ; illustrated by Patricia Casey.
— 1st U.S. ed.
p.   cm.
Summary: A young boy describes all the things he likes and
does not like about his feisty new puppy.
ISBN 0-7636-0596-4 (hardcover). — ISBN 0-7636-0597-2 (paperback)
[1 Dogs — Fiction.] I. Casey, Patricia, ill. II. Title.
PZ7.H5696Bg   1998
[E] — dc21   97-40292

10 9 8 7 6 5 4 3 2 1

Printed in Singapore

This book was typeset in AT Arta.
The pictures were done in watercolor and ink.

Candlewick Press
2067 Massachusetts Avenue
Cambridge, Massachusetts 02140

THE BEST THING ABOUT A PUPPY

CANDLEWICK PRESS
CAMBRIDGE, MASSACHUSETTS

Judy Hindley

illustrated by

Patricia Casey

The good
thing about a
puppy is,
he's warm
and
wriggly.

The bad thing is,
he won't
keep still.

The good thing is,
the way he
rolls and
bounces.

The bad thing is,
he goes and jumps
in puddles — and then
he bounces back
and shakes himself and
wants to cuddle.

The good thing is,

you get to walk him every day.

The bad thing is,

he wants to go his own way.

The good thing is, he loves to chase a ball.

The bad thing is, he hates to give it back.

The good thing is,
he likes to race
with you.

The bad thing is,

he trips you!

The good thing is,
he knows just when
to comfort you.

The bad thing is,
he licks your hands
and then your
face and neck
and ears —

shoo,
puppy!
Shoo!

Sometimes when you call, he will not come.

And then you have to call and call and look for him.

But when you find your puppy,

you're so glad!

The best thing is,
a puppy is a friend.

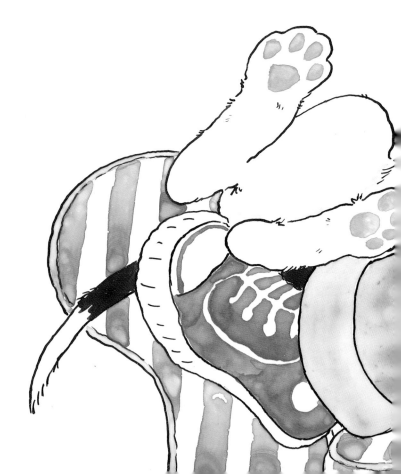

Woof! **W**oof!

Get off me, pup!

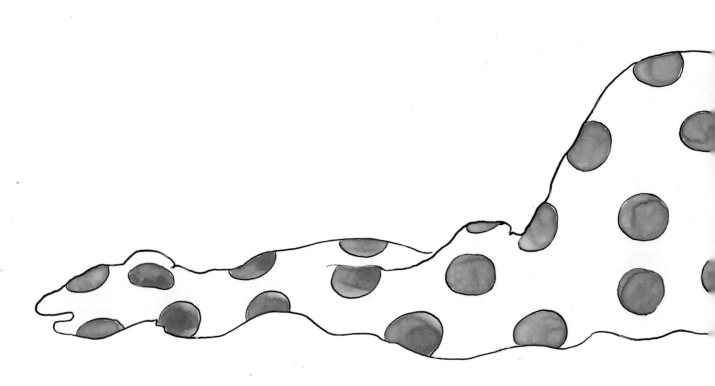